Hawk Divine

J.M. Duke

ISBN-13: 978-1-909279-04-9
ISBN-10: 1909279048

CONTENTS

1   A Light in the Darkness (Anubis)   1

2   Finding the Sun (Bast)   5

3   Architect of Truth (Thoth)   9

4   The Crest of a Phoenix (Sekhmet)   13

5   One Fire, One Eternity (Set)   17

6   Let One Song Rise (Horus)   23

7   Water and Dust Walking (Isis)   29

8   Blessed by Becoming (Osiris)   33

ACKNOWLEDGMENTS

With thanks to: Paul Stagg, for all the love, support, coffee and proofing;
To Garry and Hilda Stagg, for all your help and kindness;
To Thomas Duke, for encouraging me, one way or another;
And to JJ, Dana Varahi, and Anton Channing, for the brain food and late night philosophy.

"Hail Thoth, architect of truth,
give me words of power that when I speak the life of a man
I may give his story meaning."

- *Egyptian Book of the Dead*

A LIGHT IN THE DARKNESS

I stand on the bridge, its ancient stony surface cold and damp and deep. A thin veneer of tarmac skins primeval surfaces – a facade of modernity upon wild rock, tamed by human hands. Below me dark water flows, cutting one side of town from the other. Empty cans rattle in the gutter as cars pass me by, artificial lights tracing illusory paths in the gloom.

I am a stranger in a place I call home. Painfully anonymous, as figures lit by the glow of street lamps walk by on their way, flowing to and from nightclubs and pubs; the places we go to forget ourselves. I stand there for at least an hour, my shirt collar unbuttoned, my tie discarded. Tears are dry upon my pale cheeks. I stare into the black abyss below the black abyss of road. I listen to it calling me. I feel it waiting.

I am no coward. This is not easy.

My hands press down on the cold hard wall. I can feel my pulse begin to race as I hoist myself up and sit there, chill and wet, legs dangling into the long dark drop. My buffed designer shoes seem comical now. My expensive watch glimmers impotently. So much gaudy shell around a hollow aching shadow.

I lean forward, the night air cool in my nostrils, and I feel the loss of everything that had been missed. My heart yearns for what might have been. All my concern – for the life I had been surviving, the relationships to which I had been submitting, the empty goals, meaningless achievements and attempts to please – fades. There, underneath it all, is who I truly want to be. This moment, this choice to end it all, is the first and last authentic thing I might do for myself.

A chill rises up my spine and, as I continue to stare into the darkness, I hear the wind whisper faintly:

'Live.'

'Craven.'

'Never yours to take.'

Startled by the clarity of that last phrase I look up, brows furrowing. Then I feel a hand on my right shoulder. All becomes silent and still, the din of the traffic remote and unreal. I freeze, feeling a grip that is gentle at first but slowly tightening. I turn, tentatively, wondering how this person has come so close without my noticing. My mind races with what I will say. Then I look into his eyes.

They are fierce, like the eyes of a jackal. I try to speak but my words are lost, my attempts to get him away from me all in vain. His grip is strong and his gaze stronger. As he speaks to me his words blossom in my head, transforming into images of snakes and birds, of giant self-transforming flotillas and beings so immense I am as an ant before stars and nebulae.

'Everyone dies,' he says, his voice hoarse and powerful like the distant growl of an earthquake. 'But have you really lived? What you hold in your hands, now, in this moment is life, the most precious gift imaginable. All that you could experience, the depths to which you could know yourself, to which you could feel and understand profoundly – even if only for mere moments of awareness – these are yours and yours alone. If you fail to seek them, if you never plumb the depths of the unique instrument that you are, what was the point of you?' His eyes hold me, though I am aware of dark flesh and dark hair that starkly contrasts with that bright golden gaze. 'Everyone dies. Take this chance to truly live.'

The intensity of his stare becomes too much, overwhelmed I am compelled to turn away, as though I have been looking at the sun. I feel his hand lift from me then, and I cradle myself with my arms, gently rocking. I am overcome, now gripped by who I am and all I yearn for; I want to cry out like a new born, tangled in many conflicting emotions. I feel a terrifying sense of freedom. This choice is mine, it shows me that all of my choices were mine, and all will be. I breathe deeply, shaking, and climb down from the wall.

Traffic passes but I am alone on the bridge. Panic surges for a moment and then subsides, giving way to a strange sense of euphoria. I begin the long walk home.

I weave my way through town, through the streetlamp-lined passageways of my own becoming. I see life all around me: in people, in trees, in bricks and mortar, now starkly lit. It had all seemed so petty, and now it seems so precious. Every moment is a chance to live; every choice, part of a tapestry we can never fully comprehend. This world is stranger, deeper and more meaningful than I had previously known possible. *Who was that man?*

I walk down a brightly lit high street watching late night revellers en route home, their faces a parade of lively emotion. There is light in their eyes, a golden glimmer. *Is that him?* A fox runs from an overflowing bin nearby, some succulent prize in its jaws. My eyes follow its path into an alleyway. From the dark beyond the street lights, its body shadowy and sleek, it looks out at me with the shining eyes of a god.

FINDING THE SUN

Wearily I walk home from work, my clothes crumpled, my body aching. Night is falling and what few stars are still able to shine in the city sky begin to appear. The light of eons drowns in neon. I do this each day, six days a week. Always late, I stroll down whispering streets and through scent filled parkways. I catch sight of buses going by and I gaze through dulled windows at pale faces lit by clutched phones, like so many children gazing into our collective abyss.

I put my hands in my pockets and flex my sore shoulders as I walk along a path by a pond. Ducks and swans float along its surface or sit under arching trees by the bank, mocking me with their contentment. Pigeons are disturbed by my passing and scatter upwards, abandoning their vocal satisfaction with pecking at scraps. I kick out at them. Something writhes inside of me, rapaciously: a constant craving. It slithers through my mind, an undulating shadow cast upon my thoughts.

I hunger and I cannot be sated. I walk home from tasks that leave me starved: by glowing screens and photocopiers; by meetings with people who are sleeping even as they speak; by the pointless petty busy-work of greed and bureaucracy. We find a world of colour and we paint it grey. It is never enough. We always want more. Then we fear the loss.

Fear is the force behind every cruelty; it is what transforms life into numbers and numbers into profit. The more we crave the more we fear to lose, and with that fear we justify every cruelty with which we feed our craving. Running to stand still; suffering to avoid suffering. A better suit, a better car, a better house, a better job, a better spouse, more sex, more money, more power, more status. Let the gaping mouth inside of me open up and swallow it all, only to demand more. One more thing. One more thing. One more thing. For what?

I walk the path home and finally arrive at my front door. The key is devoured by the lock, and I step inside, dropping my coat on a hook. I hear my parents fighting; my mother craves my father's love, my father craves his own. I go back outside and sit on the back porch for hours, watching the moon rise. Suburban sprawl glows in the night.

The garden is a small fenced patch of grass surrounded by hedges. A young oak stands in one corner and I listen to the wind caress its leaves; they whisper poetry. The moon-shadow of the tree sways and my eyes finally grow heavy.

I am dreaming. A shadow woman dances in the moonlight, backlit and lithe; her movements are slow and predatory. She moves toward me, her form growing smaller as she merges with the silhouettes of hedges and sheds, eyes glinting in the dark, mad as gold. I am transfixed.

Then something else stirs in the gloom.

I awake with a start, my cat curled and purring in my lap, her warmth penetrating as my breath steams in the cold night air. I stroke her softly and cradle her tabby form, so easily loved and loving. She stretches and turns her head, a small motion filled with grace. In that moment the boundary between she and I slips away; we are two lamps lit by the same light. She is me in another life; a life lived moment to moment, free of craving.

Suddenly there is movement in the dark. With a burst an enormous black snake rushes from the bushes toward me. I jump to my feet and stare in disbelief, my back to the wall. Frozen by fear, I wonder if I am still dreaming. My cat lands softly on the grass and is immediately riled, enlarging herself, fur on end. She spits, pressing forward toward the huge creature, its form all ebony undulation and flickering tongue. I am filled with terror at the thought that it may strike. My cat is dwarfed, yet still approaches, all boldness and madness and predatory delight.

Her hiss becomes a yowl, a feline howling of protective fury. The serpent twitches, slowing, uncertain. There is a moment of silence as my cat glares defiantly into the face of doom. The snake opens its mouth, hungering, becoming impossibly large: a portal, a black hole filled with malice and terror. I fight the feeling that I am being drawn toward it and I find myself recalling many moments of pain and isolation, of repulsion and petty hatred.

My cat, however, is unperturbed, she crouches ready to pounce. The serpent rears and my fierce or foolish feline launches herself forward. As she moves she seems to grow, while the monstrous snake diminishes. I blink and see a cat-woman dancing with a shrinking serpent, all impossible liquid movement and mesmerising eyes. I blink again.

Now a huge cat stalks a tiny snake, glossy and black. She claws and bats its head as it hisses and lunges; then she pounces forward, biting into its neck. In my fear and excitement I move forward, away from the wall. Suddenly I see the scene as a whole, the moon glows behind me and my shadow stretches forward, undulating, joined to the snake now staring up at me from the grip of my cat's mouth. Its eyes gleam, piercing me like teeth.

She shakes the serpent violently and I feel it within me: my hunger, my fear, my own small cruelties. I feel it writhe through me, up my spine and into the back of my skull. It is in me to kill, to feast, to fuck, to flee; it is every buried but nonetheless present instinct, my insatiable aching desires.

The cat opens her maw and releases the snake. I find myself smiling kindly as I kneel and reach my hand toward it. The snake's jaws open again, hungering, seeming to contain an infinite space. As I stay present and calm in the face of this vast darkness it dissolves and there is nothing but light; it pours out, enveloping me. I feel the snake coiling through me again, but this time its body burns golden, white with the heat of a universe coming into being; a cat-woman dancing gracefully upon its back. She smiles and for a moment I feel content. I am not my hunger, my hunger belongs to me.

ARCHITECT OF TRUTH

Pigeons peck happily at bread and old cereal as I scoop handfuls from a paper bag. In this small patch of woodland, this chapel of trees, I sprinkle offerings at my feet. Animals and birds are easy to please. Foxes and crows will eat what my household discards. All are family to me. I smile as the birds feast before the bench I am sat upon. Its wood was once a tree. Starlings and house sparrows join the small banquet I lay out for them.

I turn to the empty space beside me and watch a form coalesce, a figure only I can see. Joggers and cyclists pass by and to them I am alone; I know I am anything but. He has the head and wings of a black ibis and the body of a man. Whether he is real or imaginary is of little concern. His form shimmers and shifts like vapour. He is welcome company, whispering words as wise as they are perceptive. He speaks to my heart. Perhaps he is my heart? I know that I know nothing with any certainty.

Smoke rises from my cigarette as the birds continue pecking. The spirit of tobacco mingles with my spirit silently, caressing the inside of my skull with soft spectral finger tips. I close my eyes and for a moment I am in a vast temple, the smell of incense surrounds me as priests make pious offerings to ancient deities carved in stone. To them words are beings, images that come to life; a written word a creature with flesh of rock: killed when struck out, deified when worshipped. Life that was spoken, written and adored into existence.

The ibis turns to me. I open my eyes and am in the woods once more, an ark of the wild adrift in a sea of city. Tall buildings loom in the distance, like colossal words of stone. I watch the bird-headed one rise regally from the bench and speak, images forming from the gentle sickle of his bill, weaving into a sheet of papyrus that unfurls between his outstretched hands. He speaks again and pictures draw themselves upon the page, flat and colourful to begin with, then gaining reality and moving with dimension and life. First I see a sleek black dog. I see it hunting images of prey soundlessly: the chase, the inky blood, the satisfaction. I see it find a mate, time speeds and I watch it raise its pups and die. I see the cycle continue, expanding outward, spilling from the yellowed paper, generations hunting, mating, dying. I see the glory of our embodied senses.

A solitary dog becomes the focus of our narrative now, sniffing its way around the page, as another image emerges from my companion's beak. I see an ape rise unsteadily onto its back legs to walk upright upon the paper, a whisper down the long curve of its maker's bill. The dog does not come to it at first, still wild and joyful as rising birds. Time speeds again and I watch the ape domesticate the dog, training it to obey its every command, teaching it to kill and even to die in service. They are strong together; a unity. Yet the ape, upright and proud, quickly begins to behave as if it is superior. Soon it is mocking the dog, beating and starving it, corrupting their partnership with strange notions born of arrogance.

'I know it all!' the ape exclaims, its words, large and bold, forming a barrier of sharp, spiky letters; they grow thickly into a fence of thorns. The ape pontificates, seeing its words appear to shape the world, seeing its assumptions come to life. At its feet the dog pants and looks on lovingly, still obedient. Around them the word-fence grows ever higher, becoming a labyrinth in which to enclose them with tunnels of doctrine and fortress walls mortared by principles, reinforced with edicts as hard as iron and every battlement jagged and crenulated by law. The ape perceives what it believes and cares only for what it can calculate. I see it create order from chaos, order that becomes a cage for that very creativity. I see the glory and the folly of the intellect.

I look on, fearful now, and my ibis companion opens his bill once more. From his tongue a bird of flame flies forth, trailing smoke and flecks of ash as it swoops in the free air above the word-prison. Bright with heat and jubilant as the dawn it flies above the ape, who fails to notice it, so enmeshed in expectations. The dog, however, rises, barking and ignoring the scowling admonishments of its simian master. The ape throws up its hands and turns its back on the dog, muttering as it stalks further into its word-prison. The dog whines, pining and listless. The lure of innocent freedom, the chance to run and roam as it desires tugs at it, and so it slips between the word-walls, through inky gaps too narrow for the ape to see. Overhead the bird is as bright as a star; the dog chases it, barking playfully, tail waving like a sail.

But soon the hound is yelping fearfully as the once faithful beast, now trapped behind high walls, becomes ever more frantic and afraid. I see a long shadow growing, spilling from the word-prison, cast by the light of the bird of flame. I see that such singular things, like every moment of our lives, are mocked by our compulsion to break down the complex and remarkable into something dull and comprehensible. I see the glory and the ferocity of the spirit. Concepts which once seemed set fast in the hard stone of certainty now writhe with teeth and jaws, rearing up around the ape; long tongues flickering with seductive ideals. The prison comes apart in fat slabs as it shatters under the strain of confrontation with the unknowable. Try as it might the ape cannot rationalise the shadows away, logic and language poor shields against their intensity. As the fortress falls the dog bounds to the ape through fallen principles and broken concepts, and both are swallowed into a dark, inky void.

Silence. I have stared in too long and now I cannot pull my gaze away. Somewhere I can hear the ape's ragged breathing and the dog's faint whimpers, intermingled. The weight of logic and language that had built up between them has crushed them, and in that moment of crisis they have become one creature, rising slowly from the dark, wet and black with ink. Their state of separation revealed as a lie, they have merged in the dark to become a single animal; more than mind and more than matter, more than instinct and more than belief. The shadows bleed into it, growing shorter with the recognition of every image of itself the ape-dog sees reflected in the oily depths. Accepting that which is base in us means accepting also that which is holy and, as the darkness spirals away the ape-dog finds itself in the presence of the bird of flame. At last the three combine, reborn, and there stands the ibis as before; a story that has told itself.

He sits before me once again, speaking shapes and colours until he fades. His form disperses: into the birds and trees, into the people passing by and the early stars above us, into the reader and the written. I take out a notebook and pen to write: of the wildwood and the city swarm; of men seeing that their soul walked with them all along; of finding truth in birdsong.

THE CREST OF A PHOENIX

My heart was broken, a feeling of overwhelming grief that can only be understood through experience. The loss of the bond to another seems as real as a near fatal wound and as slow and difficult to heal. Something seems torn from you, leaving a hollow emptiness. Who I was, by being with that other and then without, was altered forever. That is the gift that pain brings, the gift wrapped in a curse; the gift of change.

It is hard to tell the broken hearted that they will mend. It is hard to know it as an initiation, that the torment will end and there will be wholeness again. Something new, strong and triumphant will laugh at the memory. We cling to the void where something was and is no more, instead of seeing a space for new life to grow. We cling to the pain that could transform us, instead of allowing it. Suffering can feel powerful at times. It is easy to pass on the poisonous sting, to wield it, shut ourselves off and lash out – to pretend we are not human; we are not capable of hurting. Such self deception is the worst form of deceit, the mother of delusion. Pain embraced can burn away our illusions, allowing our perceptions to be cleansed.

My days had become robotic, letting the simple programmes run: wake, work, eat, and try to sleep; do anything but think, anything but feel. I was numb, running to stand still, to escape that cleansing walk through fire, the necessary pain that would burn my gratuitous misery to ash. My nights were haunted struggles; it was harder to push the agony away. In darkness, in sober silence, we truly face the twisted knots and jagged wounds within ourselves. My nights were filled with that face, with our joys and sorrows, with all my self-loathing at the loss.

Then one evening I slipped away into vibrant dreams, of a strange bright plateau where a huge golden lioness suckled me with two ginger kittens. I had never known such succulence, such adoration, such warmth. Her fur was soft, like balmy tender clouds. Her milk seemed to permeate my very being with love. As the kittens drank they grew, until they too were lions, silky and fair. I turned, creamy lipped, and watched them bound away under a reddening sky.

The lioness rose and for a moment seemed to eclipse the world; so golden, so adoring, her body lustrous and powerful. She gazed at me lovingly with her huge heat-filled eyes, and then bid me, without words, to climb upon her back. I rode her through hot sand dunes, padding silently to a baroque building carved into the side of a tall cliff, its walls of baked terracotta lined with pillars and looming statues of fierce beasts.

Within was a great banquette hall, the walls painted with scenes and writings alien to me. The stone table in the middle was long, covered in ornate carvings inlaid with gold. Upon it sprawled a huge feast that made my mouth water to see. Fruit and fish and meat prepared in many delicious ways, all gathered around a centre piece that took my breath away. Horror mingled with heartache, my pulse racing. The one who broke my heart lay naked on a tray, figs and grapes in upturned hands, honey glaze upon their skin.

I slid from the back of the lioness then, walking forward, filled with disbelief and a strange creeping hunger. I turned back and gazed into those huge warm eyes and as I watched she glittered, cracked and fell apart. It was as though she were made of many tiny mirrors and now they buzzed and thronged, like fish or bees, becoming spirals and mandala, flattening and swarming before me. I stared at my reflection and watched it transform.

My eyes became huge and gold, my body contorting, clothes ripping open. From my hands and feet I sprouted paws and claws. This strange metamorphosis was surprisingly pleasant, as though I had always been wearing the wrong skin. I became the lioness, I became the mirror swarming.

I looked down at myself, all muscle and fur. I felt strength course through me and a now overwhelming hunger. I turned and leapt upon the table, devouring my former lover piece by bloody piece. The meat was so warm and tender, I was completely engrossed in the feast. I remembered betrayal, the taste was bitter on my tongue; I remembered our lack of kindness and how we used each other for fun. I remembered many things as bones cracked and skin ripped. As I felt it all digest inside of me, I could see through their eyes. There had been so much hurt clenched inside - all fleshy red, like dragon skin - as if hell were never really a place, but something we carry deep within. All our fears and doubts and withheld yearning.

As I lay upon the table, thoroughly gorged, I felt my fur begin to smoulder and tears begin to fall. These tears were made of sparking fire, cried for all my fears, for every doubt and longing from which I had been hiding. I knew, in that moment, I could never hide from such things again. I spoke them out loud - a liberating chant - each tear burning like a star in my orbit before fizzling away, released. Then, as if someone were speaking through me, I heard myself say:

'We were such wounded creatures, like birds with broken wings that longed to fly. We punished each other for our inadequacies, instead of finding joy in our existence.'

And with that my fuming body burst in to scorching golden fire. I felt the last of what I had clung to crumble, ashen: my arrogance, my desire. I became a searing white ball of heat and that heat became my heart. I stood, a child again, reborn in a blazing, pulsing egg of light. Great wings unfurled from my shining heart and butterflies of flame burst from my mouth. I was essence, a purity anything other than naive or weak; the potential in each moment for apotheosis.

Pain had broken me: like an egg cracking open, a seed bursting forth, a cocoon ripping. The wound that sets the light free. It was always in me.

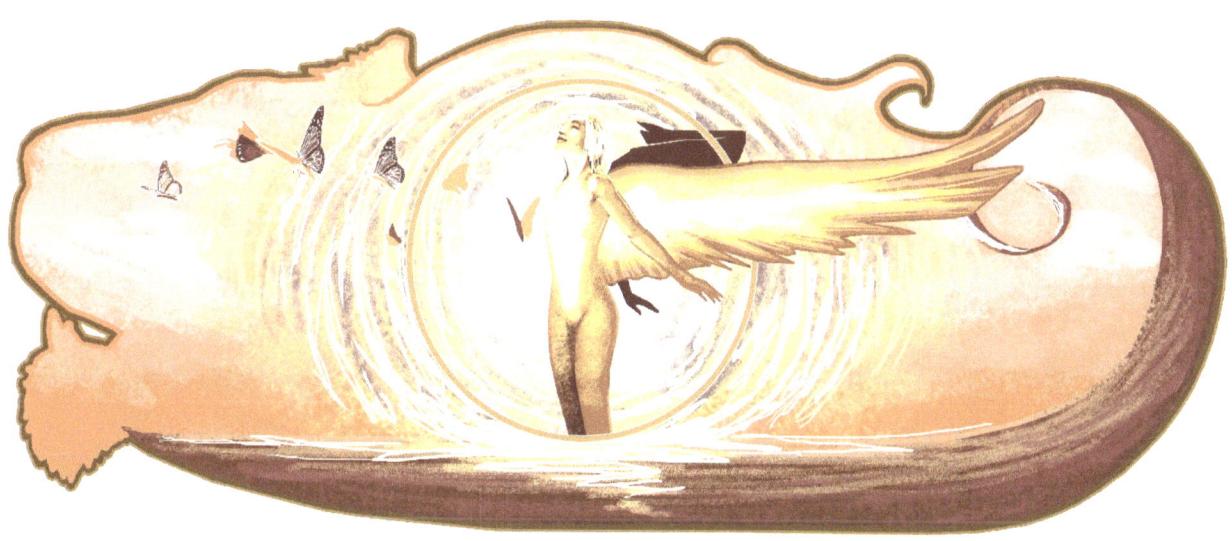

ONE FIRE, ONE ETERNITY

I am a vain and foolish creature, seeking enlightenment. This is the story of my folly.

All my life I sought self-perfection, in unwise ways for unwise reasons. I yearned to throw off my needs and weaknesses, to become something godlike and invulnerable to this world. I filled myself with ideas and ideals, with illusions and delusions, inflating and making emptier a naive and fragile sense of self. I found comfort in this, in thinking myself superior, rather than simply afraid.

For so long I found the actions of others wanting. Hungry for perfection, I was all too willing to sit in judgement. The outer world seemed full of greed and deceit. I felt surrounded by fools who were so easily hypnotised by neon magicians wielding empty slogans and lies, viciously protecting worlds of words, while pillaging and destroying the tangible world and its fragile life.

I would walk alone in the city at night, basking in my isolation. In the small dark hours it briefly belonged to owls and foxes and moths hunting moonlight. In the day I walked the scarred remains of forests, green tracks between mammoth concrete highways, each passageway a desert oasis. I resisted indoctrination into a reality I could not accept among people to whom I could not relate. If being like them was what it was to be human then I was alien, a gentle interloping creature in disguise as a person.

I watched others bent, twisted, moulded into shape by the rewards and punishments of social acceptance, by the functions and masks of a culture that seemed evil to me. I withdrew further. I lost myself to meditation like an addict to the needle, seeking to numb the pain of my isolation with yet more isolation. I deluded myself that my escapism was illumination, that the physical world was only a shadow of that which held true meaning. In meditation I encountered a spirit beyond all things that seemed so obviously separate and superior. It drew me away into its perfect light and each time I returned to a world so illusory and flawed, filled will sorrow and pain and petty human beings. How could they fail to see the beauty beyond their trivial sufferings?

I abstained from meat and other substances, then became celibate. I took pride in my purity, in my lack of connection to a material world I now held in contempt. Even the wild places seemed less and less holy to me, filled with death and sex and torment. I confined myself in my home like a monk in a temple. I found myself wondering if I should ever leave. I could sit in meditation, fasting, and just be. I could renounce this world.

I remember the night I sat in meditation, quietly ready to be free; ready to fully dissociate from reality. I felt and saw the light above, I let it flow through me. As I watched my thoughts drift like clouds and clear from the sky of my mind something unfamiliar began to stir. There was darkness seeping upwards, darkness from within, it refused to dissipate and began to consume me.

I snapped awake, shaking and disturbed. My inner sanctum had ceased to be a safe haven. Unable to stay away from my one and only sanctuary, night and day I delved back into that space, reaching for the light, and the brighter it became the blacker was the dark. It pulled at me with teeth and claws, threatening to rip me limb from limb, to consume me in a chasm of fear; a pit of ebony scales flecked with lightning. I felt forsaken, cast out of my Eden. I felt fatally flawed and ashamed.

I had lost my refuge from the world; I was forced, inch by painful inch, to face reality. I began walking at night again, looking up at the stars and staying out to watch the sun rise. I had thought myself better than this world, this beautiful, incomparable wonder. I had shunned wind through trees, starlings in flight, the crisp tingle of frost. Who was I to judge this?

I observed other people wandering, going about their lives. They too I had rejected, and far more readily. I had been so quick to judge and disparage them when I could only judge myself - they might lie to each other, but self deception was worse. Without my refuge I quickly realised how much pain and sorrow I had been hiding from. I cried for hours in isolation. I sat in parks and squares and cafes and was comforted just to be with people. I saw beauty in my mother's eyes, even as she scolded me. I saw compassion in my brother's actions, even as he mocked me. I saw nobility in the small things people do for one another, even as they hurt each other. I saw that my judgement was just an opinion, a perspective, a guess. How was I any better than anyone else?

I wondered if everyone felt this darkness inside, if all of us were trying to hide away from something in ourselves – if we each face our own personal abyss. Just as night defines day and roots define branches, this shadow had defined me. I was humbled. I was grateful.

I remember well the other night, sometime after my first encounter with the darkness. Once more I sat in meditation, focussed on my breath. Once more the darkness came for me and I smiled, looking deeply into it. I let it swallow me into its giant serpent mouth, and inside I saw myself. I saw all of my fears and my outrageous lies; everything that disgusted me about myself. I laughed. I saw how I had observed these things in others and the world, and as I came to know this I gently forgave them and myself. Then at last I saw my perfectly imperfect greatness hiding in the dark, like butterflies made of fire it fluttered up, shining. Until, finally, in that shadow place there was nothing left. My body gave a shudder of relief, then, with a flash of light, I was released.

Out of the darkness I came spilling with all these things I had been hiding from myself, and I saw a colossal figure spearing open the dark mouth. His skin was scaled, the colour of shadow, dancing with veins of lightning, and his head was bestial – almost draconic. His wicked weapon struck with repeated ferocity, until the darkness twisted and shrank away. At last it was the size of a python; the shadow-man bent and let it crawl up his arm in undulating coils. He kissed it when it reached him, then from his shoulders it hung, obedient and deadly.

'It takes darkness to face darkness,' his bass voice rumbled; his eyes like white hot coals. This man was otherness incarnate: the enemy, the shadow, the one through whom I could know myself truly. He was all I could ever find undesirable, all I could never stand or be; he was all I denied but was in truth or potential. I nodded, my arms opening, knowing that in his embrace I would be liberated from my own ignorance – I would know and own my capacity for evil. He stepped forward into me, disappearing into my skin, as though I were water and he a stone. I accepted him.

Then I felt a great flutter in my chest and I sensed something pouring through me, filling me, overflowing from the crown of my head. Rapidly I was thrown into something unimaginable, a vortex of galaxies and nebulae that spiralled, vast and unfathomable. I was at once the whole of it and an infinitesimally small part, a tiny, momentary flicker in a vast fire of aware substance. It was everything and it was alive, dark and light and spiralling. Infinite moments experienced in infinite lives, one vast awareness with countless senses and countless eyes.

Then I heard the booming voice of the shadow-man again, I heard myself also saying the words as I came back to my senses. 'Know this: you are no better or worse, you are simply here in this life – this gift – and in every moment you must be both ready to die and ready to live. We are each singular flames rising from the same searing consciousness.'

I am a vain and foolish creature, seeking enlightenment. This was the story of my folly, and my awakening.

LET ONE SONG RISE

It is a long hot hike through the forest. I have left the main road far behind and biting insects swarm at my face when the breeze drops, buzzing in my ears. I soldier on, undeterred. It rained earlier. I find peace in the earthy smell that has followed the downpour, and the rising sound of birdsong. A haze of sunlight streams through the trees, creating a show of slowly dancing silhouettes on the damp, leafy earth; shadows that look like long spindly arms covered in tiny wings.

I am heading to a cabin in the hills, a place to be alone in the wild. Of course, you are never alone in the wild, but the absence of people can be good for the spirit and the mind. There is a sense of being centred in oneself that comes from time in wilderness, a connection with something primal and strong. Out here it is easy to love the sun burning bright in the sky, and in so doing know the sun that burns bright in the heart, as well as the shadows that both cast.

I trek most of the day through trees and hills and pastures, briefly stopping for lunch. As I sit by a stream dappled with light I watch a falcon soar in the warm blue heights above. It is golden in the sunshine and the sight of it fills me with elation, as if by watching it I too take flight. I walk on.

It is a pleasant journey and normally uneventful. However, just a few miles from the cabin I hear twigs snapping near the path on which I walk and I have the distinct feeling I am being watched. I walk for some time, unable to shake the feeling of a presence. Though I look and listen carefully I find myself ostensibly alone.

A little further on I hear strange music in the trees, like a piper playing a slow, haunting melody, accompanied by a drumming beat. I turn and look deep into the wood and as I do so a figure steps out under the trees a little way ahead of me. I am shocked, it is as if I am staring at my own reflection, but when I hesitantly wave the other simply watches before, with a smile, slowly returning the gesture. We stare at each other then until, with a step, the other is gone, out of sight.

I move quickly along the path, all curiosity and panic. I look for the other, seeing no one, until, on further still, a figure steps out onto the path ahead, lit from behind by the setting sun. This time it is a stranger, a man with the head of peregrine falcon. I stop in my tracks. The forest will play tricks on the mind but this is the strangest I have ever encountered. Is this a fairy, or some kind of extraterrestrial? Is it a man in a mask trying to trick me? The blinking of his huge dark eyes makes me put aside any thoughts of masks.

'Are you a spirit? Am I welcome here?' I wonder as I stare at him.

'I am a god among spirits', his voice whispers in my mind in reply. 'And it is you who has welcomed me.' He bows to me then, low and gracefully, then jumps into the air, shape shifting. In several flashing motions there is a falcon flying above. I stand, frozen with astonishment. Have I just imagined the past hour?

I hasten to the cabin, my body tingling with a strange mixture of fear and elation. For days all is normal; I read by the fire, chop wood, run in the forest and meditate. I almost begin to forget the strange encounter. Then, one morning, as I leave the cabin to run through the trees, I find him standing outside, waiting for me. My mind races and my body is frozen with bewilderment as I gaze into those huge dark eyes. He says nothing, but with a gesture of his pale hand he beckons me to follow him.

He guides me to a clearing of soft grass. All around us birds flutter in the shadows. As a peregrine he soars above me while I lay against the rough bark of a great oak. I watch him circle and I follow his wanderings, my mind drifting in and out of focus, like ripples on a pond slowly settling. This place was here long before me and would be here long after I was gone. Yet I feel connected. The bird song, the vibrant green, feels as though it is part of me. Nature has many eyes that turn us back upon ourselves. My mind stills, its waters at once reflecting the sky and revealing their depths. As I watch this strange god fly I feel his strength course through me - graceful and powerful - and I can just make out that strange music; his music. It is in everything, connecting everything.

'Close your eyes,' I hear him whisper, and I do. 'Open the eye within; see with light, with purpose, with passion in defiance of oblivion.'

It is as though a thousand eyes open inside of me, like the many and varied facets of a kaleidoscopic jewel. Simultaneously I look inside myself and outside myself and I can no longer see the difference. The many eyes overlap, becoming one great golden orb, blazing from me and upon me, taking its candid measure. It seems to approve and I hear the bird-god speak again:

'Let one song rise from you: the song of the beginning, the song of manmade palaces in god made Eden, of order in chaos and chaos in order; harmony woven by wisdom and demons bound by understanding.'

Without warning the golden eye flies forth into my chest, spearing my heart. My body trembles with the power of it, overwrought with an onslaught of visions.

I am flying, soaring over a city at night, a billion stars are reflected in a billion lights below. I race downward. Moonlight shines, coiling into deep shadows; shadows that writhe and birth monsters. Through windows I watch demons stalk the dreams of twitching sleepers. Of those awake many stare, transfixed, into violent horrors on phones and TV screens. Some cry in dark corners, enveloped by darker claws; some rage into the night; some numb themselves with pills and potions; some smile twisted smiles. The darkness cloaks all of them, sinking its teeth in. But there are others.

In the night I see pockets of light beating against the dark. Mothers soothing, fathers protecting; dreamers imagining, artists creating. I see people nurturing, speaking, singing, sculpting, acting, dancing, the light of their hearts into the world. Sharing their souls boldly in the face of monsters. Their hearts are the stars in the night below.

As these lights grow they shine onto others, and they too are lit up in their turn. The light of civilisation spreads through the darkness of ignorance; consciousness blossoms from primal anguish. The sun rises on a world of manmade wonder entwined with nature's beauty, for nature is only as monstrous as the secrets we keep from ourselves.

It is our birthright and our duty to find that light within, to know the song of our beginning and our becoming. We are mad creatures that must elevate ourselves, born of impulse into tragedy we can wallow or we can fly. Our civilisations stand and fall on our capacity to cultivate the crop of consciousness, our ability to sow and to harvest wisdom, without which we are the mere puppets of our own demons.

I open my eyes and find myself sitting beneath the tree. Something stirs within me. From my soul the hawk divine will soar, my winged heart a warrior.

WATER AND DUST WALKING

I walk by a winding river, watching daylight play in bright sparks upon its rippling surface. Willow trees bow by its side, sheltering singing birds. The sun warms its water as swallows swoop over it, snatching insects from the air; their playful twittering a prayer to the sky. People pass me by. Unseen, I watch them and smile. I am a student of all nature: human, wild, divine. I watch the faces of people, of clouds, of the waters. I observe the city in the distance, its spires towering over the trees. The river ebbs and flows, like our joys and sorrows.

All things pass and change. It is important to let go of thinking otherwise. There is only one revolution that matters, the revolution of the mind. You are yourself, with all your small troubles. You are the leading edge of a process that has been going on for billions of years. You are so concerned for your safety. You were once in the hearts of stars. You are full of hopes and fears. You are water and dust walking.

I walk by a river of chance and change, witnessing a great spirit at play in many forms. Each drop of water, each feather, each child's smile, behind them something reaches out. Can you see? I watch the flight of a swallow to her nest and see her hungry children sated. I see the flight of a falcon and the life of a swallow taken. The river carries on its course, different drops creating the same stream. A man shouts into his phone, his heart is pounding. If the world is a stage, he is so very immersed in his part. He believes he is real in a dream.

I walk to a grassy space and meet with many friends. There is food and drink and laughter in the sunlight. As I eat I think of swallows. As I drink I think of the river. There is talk of many things; of ideas and ideals, of people and their shoes, of pretty clothes and ugly truths. There is amusement and argument. A human twittering prayer. Two friends begin to beat on drums and another shakes a rattle. I watch as people dance, creating a spectacle to match the rhythm. They move like butterflies and bees. I get up to join them, my body so many expressions without words. I open my arms and look up into the sky.

As I move I feel I am a tree filled with chattering sparrows, then a dandelion seed floating in the wind. I am rooted, then uplifted: feather, moss, then stone. My bare feet tingle as I spin on the warm grass. I hear a guitar join the rhythm. I am a buzzard circling high in the sky. I am worms wriggling in the roots of wild garlic. I am a droplet of morning dew trembling in a spider's web.

As I move my body to the playful tune I am lost in all this wonder, I feel life pulsing through me. I spin and spin and spin, rocked in the arms of a goddess. Her hair is forest thousands of miles wide, her skin a desert at sunrise. The oceans of the world pulse in her veins and she smiles. Oh how she smiles! Sirius sparkles in her eyes. From her womb spirals out the evolution of life, like a polyp; countless tendrils of countless creatures birthing and dying into each other, like every cell in my own singular finite form.

I slow my movements, making my way from the other dancers to sink and leisurely lie in the grass as the music continues. The sky is filled with birds and my body with elation. I wiggle my fingers in front of my face and wonder at the life in them. One day I will die and descend into this earth. I will rise as spring flowers to feed butterflies. I am a ripple and I am the river. We are all echoes of each other, echoing into eternity.

I gather myself and say goodbye to my friends. The day is cooling. I walk back to the river and sit on a bench by the bank. Joggers run past, bodies reveling in exertion, like spring lambs chasing each other in green pastures. The water stirs and I feel *her*; something that transcends this world and takes its myriad parts higher. I watch her rise from the water, a woman in a red dress crowned with a golden serpent coiled around a throne. Only I have eyes to see this, the water slides away from her without a sound. She is so bright, her smile intoxicating. She is a woman, but she is more. She is *Woman*, archetypal and ineffable. I could die looking into her eyes. She raises her feathered arms - such colourful wings - as if asking me to embrace her. Then she whispers strange words that spark into life from her tongue, objects that spin and fill with colour spill from her lips and weave their way toward me, each becoming a different bird. Their strange language too seems to whisper something into life, something just beyond our senses.

Then she herself bursts into many colours that become a flock of swallows leaping skyward. I grin as I see their joyous flight and then I turn my gaze once more to the water. A woman and her child walk by, glancing furtively at me. I know that I must seem strange. As if anything in this world is ordinary, and why would we want it to be? Where is the magic in that?

I walk on into sunset and watch the sky burn. Trees and distant buildings turn gold and then crimson before darkness comes. I watch birds flock to sleep in trees and a fox scurries across my path. There is only one revolution that matters, the revolution of the mind. This close to the city it is hard to see the river of stars that is the reflection of earth in heaven above, just as, immersed in ourselves, it is hard to see our divinity.

BLESSED BY BECOMING

All is darkness. I do not know where I am. Now and then I think I can see stars in the cold blackness, but when I try to focus on them they disappear. Then I see a bright light far off in the distance. Dazed, I walk towards it. It illuminates a long dark corridor through the gloom. I walk for what seems like an eternity and eventually I reach a tall narrow doorway. It hums with power. White patterns adorn its edges, moving slowly and symmetrically. I've never seen anything like this before.

I cannot see anything beyond the hot white light shining through the doorway, but I feel a presence. I do not know how or why, but I know I am being watched, assessed even. I wait, nervously, and slowly the light cools. I peer in through the doorway. Though I am afraid I am also compelled to enter. I step inside.

I am in a large brightly lit kitchen. I smell bread, cakes and honey. I feel warmth from a fireplace. A long countertop runs along a window ledge that takes up the entire back wall. Through the large windows I see a verdant garden; flowers bloom and trees hang with fruit. It is green in a way I feel I have dreamed about, but I cannot recall when. Countless butterflies flit between flowers. I hear a chair creak and become conscious that I am staring out of the window and have completely missed the fact that there is someone else in the room with me. I turn.

An old man sits in front of the fireplace; steam from a hot cup of tea held in his wrinkled hands gently swirls upward, a soft focus kaleidoscope. His skin is deeply tanned. He purses his lips and blows gently on the water before taking a slow sip. Then he looks up at me with gentle golden-brown eyes. His voice is soft yet powerful.

'I was like you once. I did as I was told, giddily believed in the world presented to me. I was so eager to fit in to it all: to slide into the processes around me and belong to them, to be good, to be unwavering, to be beloved. Then I died. An experience beyond words, beyond the mundane awareness of time and space.'

I try to speak and find I cannot. The man places his tea on a nearby table and stands. He cocks his head to one side and smiles at me in a fatherly way. Then he looks me over as if taking the measure of me. Light from the garden shines on him, making parts of his skin glow green, then white.

'Beauty, joy and wonder should not be swept away for some other day. That day may never come. Every moment is a choice: embrace this wonder or deny it; love what you have or fear it; surrender and be light as a feather, or crave and cling and be weighed down like a stone.' He pauses, stroking his short beard, then looks away from me into the garden. 'Fear will tell you to close yourself, to run and hide. Sometimes this is advisable, but not when it blinds you, not when you are running and hiding from the truth. Then the truth becomes a burden. It makes your heart heavy, and the heart was made to be light, to have wings. How else can the soul fly?'

House sparrows burst from the bushes by the windows, dozens of them. I am filled with joy as I watch them scatter into the trees. I feel something flutter in my chest. A large ginger cat walks out from under the windows and pads languidly across the grass. The old man turns to me again.

'Love will tell you to open yourself, to know who and what we really are. Sometimes this is not advisable, but when we isolate ourselves all the universe seems meaningless and savage. Then we make it so. We must open our eyes to our creating, to the role that we ourselves play in the making of our stories, and both the good and the evil we permit in them. Even an evil man can unburden his heart and be redeemed if he is willing to see his folly; that to crush another is to crush yourself.' He raises an eyebrow and looks to the garden again.

I see something stir by an apple tree, a dark shadow is cast against the sunlight as a man stands from where he had been sitting just out of sight. His skin is black as night; his eyes like white hot coals. *What is this place?* The thought races through me as I look away, but I am strangely calm. The old man continues to speak.

'When you rise from death it changes you. You have touched more reality than most are prepared to face. Though all must. All do. You will gather yourself, thought and bone, and know that all the universe is but one magnificent beating heart. One thing becoming infinite things, forever.'

He turns to face me and suddenly the entire scene is ripped away. I stare into the blazing eyes of an enormous shining being made of light in the blackness of space. My whole body is thrown forward into his open arms, into his chest. It is as though his heart is the entire universe, a glorious starry explosion of life. Doorway after doorway appear all around me as I speed through a space that seems to warp in on itself. Through each door I see a moment in a life through the eyes of another. They are countless. I am myself and I am somehow all of them. I am wholeness. I am brightness. I am the joyful spiralling of everything at once.

'But it is not your time.' Abruptly I am back in the kitchen, dazed once more. The old man's hand is on my right shoulder. He smiles broadly and I notice then beyond him, across the room from me, is a set of scales. A beating human heart balances against a feather. I know, without knowing how, that it is mine. I look down at my chest then. There is a dark neatly cut cavity. As I stare at it a single large golden butterfly emerges. I hold out my hand and it flutters to it, landing on my index finger.

'It is time, however, for you to know that there is so much more to this world. That there is so much more to you.' The butterfly flutters up and with a bright flash it is a golden hawk. It rushes and flutters around the room and calls to me, disappearing through the bright doorway through which I had entered. I follow it into the light. 'Wake up.' I hear the old man say. 'You are alive!'

JANICE DUKE

ABOUT THE AUTHOR

Janice Duke is an illustrator, speaker and writer born in East-London. She now lives in the Highlands of Scotland. She is primarily interested in art and philosophy based topics, strongly influenced by a master's degree in philosophy with a focus on aesthetics and environmental ethics. Nature, mythology, psychology and the exploration of consciousness inspire and inform her work.

For more information see www.janiceduke.com